HAVE A WITCHIN' HOWL-O-WEEN

Shiftmas, The Sequel

A SMUTACULAR WITCHY SHIFTER NOVELLA
BOOK II

S. P. ICEY

WITCHIN' VIBES
(WRITING PLAYLIST)

Down on Me by Jeremih, 50 Cent
Like You Mean It by Steven Rodriguez
The Devil Wears Lace by Steven Rodriguez
Cyclone by Baby Bash
Slayer by Bryce Savage
Gas Pedal by Sage the Gemini
RUNRUNRUN by Dutch Melrose
That's My Girl by Fifth Harmony
Body Language by Jesse McCartney, T-Pain
Bumble Bee by Bambee
He's Not Real by PansyVibes
A Little More by Ed Sheeran
Strawberries & Cigarrettes by Troye Sivan
Go Girl by PitBull

CONTENT WARNINGS

This novella contains adult themes including but not limited to violence, gore, magic, on page adult scenes, sexual acts such as oral sex, public sex, vaginal sex.

Mental health is very important, so please if any of the aforementioned triggers could be a sensitive read or topic, proceed with caution.

Cover Designed by S. P. Icey

Formatting by S. P. Icey

Line & Copy Editing by @maraseditingservices on Instagram

Proofreading by @maraseditingservices on Instagram

Paperback ISBN 9798990548596

CONTENTS

❧ I ☙

ALASTOR

Ten months.

It had been ten months since those filthy flea infested mutts snatched her.

My mate.

My witch.

I searched high and low. Every known den, run down building, entire forests.

And she was nowhere to be found.

I was at my wits end. My soul broke with each day that dragged by without her. The beast within yowled constantly. His thirst for blood, for revenge, was nearly untamed.

The attacks increased. The wolves were on a violent rampage and growing increasingly more difficult to hide.

The leads I had, vanished without a trace.

I remained at a standstill with no hope in sight.

That was, until the week prior to All Hallows' Eve.

My nightly patrol had been uneventful once more, lacking any signs of new activity. I retraced my steps, landing myself at the stoop of my missing witch's cottage. Pressing the hidden latch on my belt, her wards unsealed and the front door slowly opened as I stepped over the threshold.

The latch was a trinket I had commissioned by an old friend decades before to aid in my line of work. When one works in the supernatural's equivalent of the FBI— the Supernatural Department of Worldwide Security—such gadgets come in handy. Especially if I ever had a rather...reluctant informant or suspect. Which, most of them were. If we didn't get the answers we were in search of, we were encouraged to tie up loose ends in whichever way we deemed fit. More often than not, leading to a satisfying death of said individual.

Once I got ahold of the mutts who had stolen my witch, only the most gruesome fate would be satisfactory. Only, of course, once Maeli was safe and back in my arms.

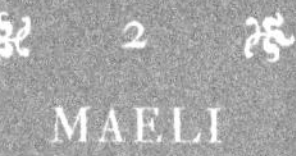

MAELI

I lost track of how long the flea ridden assholes held me captive in their shithole of a den. I'd also lost track of the amount of fights that broke out on a daily basis between the testosterone fueled wolves. It was like I was thrown into a pen of overcompensating bodybuilders doped up on steroids.

My head was constantly pounding from the noise. The fact that it hadn't driven me to total insanity was a godsdamned miracle.

They kept me drugged and unconscious ninety percent of the time, only allowing me to wake for meals and bathroom breaks. And unfortunately, whatever they pumped into my system...blocked me from accessing my magic. It was as if there was an invisible wall between my psyche and my power. I was utterly useless.

I succumbed to memorizing every square inch of my cement block cell in addition to the wolves who came and went. They rotated a different wolf on guard for the first chunk of my time here. After twenty rotations, they started again. In the same order. I watched their every movement, every little tick or twitch, waiting for a weakness and biding my time until the perfect opportunity came.

Today was apparently that day.

My target was a younger wolf. His facial features weren't as worn, as refined, as some of the more mature ones. He wore a small empathetic smile whenever he'd enter my cage, bringing with him my meal or a change of clothes. The others simply scowled and flashed their hatred with no attempt at hiding their feelings about me being a witch. Or witches in general. They taunted me with slurs, smacked me around, hit me, kicked me bloody. But not this one.

He was maybe in his late thirties by human standards. Barely an adult by wolf standards. Maybe that was why he seemed to have a soft spot for me. Maybe by some chance he hadn't learned to hate us yet. The older they got, the slower they aged and the faster their hatred built. No different than the shifters.

Alastor.

My chest wrenched at the thought of him. The panther shifter. The one who would've killed me if he'd been like any of the others. The one who I'd started to fall for before these douche canoes kidnapped me off the doorstep of my cottage in the woods.

Snap out of it!

I shook my head, clearing the heartthrob from my mind. I needed to be ready. This would be my only chance.

I sat curled on the thin mattress that was shoved into the far corner of my cell and nailed to the floor.

The wolf opened the gate and padded in. He was in his human form this time instead of his russet wolf. He brought me dinner—a la frozen entree.

I forced out a sob, hiding my face in my hands. His footsteps paused. "Are you okay?" he asked, worry etched in his tenored voice.

Good.

I squeezed my eyes together and willed a few tears to fall, streaking my cheeks and pooling into the palms of my hands. "I just...it's been—" another choked sob"—I don't know. I miss my family."

The mattress suddenly shifted as he sat on the floor next to me. "You have a family?"

"Just...just my sister." I sniffled. "I'm all she has left. And now...I've been in here for Gods knows how long."

It wasn't a complete lie. Kali was like a sister to me.

Take the bait. Come on.

He scooted close and slung his arm over my shoulders. "I know what you mean. I haven't seen my family in years."

Okay, I'm really going to feel like an asshole now.

"Really?" I glanced up, turning my head toward him as I slowly batted my wet lashes. Sympathy rang in his silver eyes.

But I need to get out.

They'll only keep me alive for so long before they get bored and kill me.

The wolf leaned in, giving me the perfect opportunity. I tilted my head, and his eyes fluttered close, lips pursing.

Now.

I reared back and smacked my head against his as hard as I could. "I'm sorry," I whispered as his head fell backward with his palm clutching his forehead. I shot up, blinking away the spots that danced in my vision. He let out a groan and I kicked him straight in the nards. "I'm really sorry, but I can't stay here any longer." I hurried, snatching the key ring from his belt loop as he howled and I ran toward the gate.

I fumbled with the keys as I tried to find the right one for my cell. The wolf continued to howl behind me, alerting the others. Paws pounded overhead, heading straight to my cinder block hell hole. Sweat slicked my neck as panic clenched its boned fingers around my throat. I was running out of time. My hands shook and I dropped the key ring.

Come on!

I shoved the first key my fingers touched into the padlock and turned. It clicked open, and the lock hit the floor with a dull tink. Pushing open the gate, I bolted down the dirt and stone corridor. My bare feet thudded against the ground as I ran through cavern after cavern until the sounds of oversized pounding paws disappeared behind me.

Finally, I came to a stop where a hint of sunlight streaked along the ground ahead. I pushed down the excited relief that was banging in the base of my stomach. Cracks dotted the dirt wall ahead of me. I stopped in my tracks.

This is it.

I took a step back, sucked in a breath, and sprinted forward, barreling through the wall and to my freedom. Rubble crashed around me. I glanced quickly over my shoulder as I kept running. The hole behind me grew as more and more dirt crumbled to the ground around it. I kicked it into high gear, pushing myself harder, faster.

Trees flew past me, branches smacked me on the face, chest, and legs as I ran by. Pure fresh oxygen flowed through my lungs.

Free.

I'm free!

I broke from the treeline at the edge of a cliff. Miles and miles of woodland-covered mountains spanned ahead. It was beautiful for about zero-point-five seconds before I realized the breathtaking view stood between me and my escape from dog-men hell. A strangled, slightly crazed laugh fell from my lips.

I am so fucked.

❧ 3 ❧

ALASTOR

I awoke to a slew of howls filling the night. It was utterly deafening.

As I rolled out of bed, Maeli's fair complexion drifted into my mind. A flash of a heart-stopping smile graced her features. Then within a blink of an eye, fear, blood, and despair.

Fire licked at my subconscious and the beast within me roared. My body hummed with adrenaline as spots of red blotted my vision. Limbs split, burning as they tore apart, only to be fused together again. A series of cracks popped beneath the fur sprouting along my body. Within painful seconds, the beast lunged forward, replacing my human form. We took off with a single train of thought between us.

Mate.

My paws pounded against the forest floor. Leaves and sticks crunched beneath my heavy weight. A wolf's scent lingered in the air and the blood in my veins began to boil at the offense. I slowed my pace, readying for the hunt. My paws were as silent as the night stars that were due to make their appearance within a few hours. Nearly the entirety of the day was spent desperately in search of my witch.

The panting of the mongrel parted the evening breeze. I was growing closer to my target. My paws lightly padded along the ground, not a sound evident. My heavy breath slowed as I narrowed in on the wolf.

Now.

I launched through the brush with my claws extended, thirsty for their victim. My mouth watered at the thought. My jaw locked around the russet fur at the nape of its neck, eliciting a howl from the long-haired beast.

The male's howl fell to a whimper as he quickly cowered to the forest-ridden floor. His paws rubbed against his large ears in an attempt to cower.

This one must be new.

Unlike myself and other shifters, the wolves were not born with their abilities out of the womb. Once they achieved full maturity in their human bodies, which more often than not was between their twenty-fifth and twenty-sixth years of life, they experienced their first shift. It was a vicious transformation, one their packs prepared them for throughout the entirety of their youth. Wolves were alone in this. Panthers, foxes, lions, and the like, were born with our shifting abilities, albeit still painful when we first transform, it's not remotely the same level as the mutts. And perhaps that was why my kind were far more in touch with our beasts and maintained more control.

I released a growl when the wolf tried to escape. His movement stopped, becoming utterly still. He whimpered again after a few moments passed. I unclamped my jaw and set him free. He wasted no time, twisting so his back was no longer exposed to me, his teeth glared in the evening light and his pupils narrowed into grey slits.

A deep hiss slithered passed my jowls and he stood down. An odd look glinted within his eyes. The pit of my stomach churned.

The wolf sat on his haunches. Then within a blink of an eye, the russet fur, large paws, and canine body disappeared. In its place stood his human flesh, pale as the nearly full moon with short bedraggled locks aflame upon his head.

The wolf held his hands up with his palms facing me. I narrowed my stare in return, cautious. "I mean no harm. Please."

Lies.

I shifted and returned to my human body as well. Anger rippled beneath my skin, ready to pounce at any moment. "Where is she?" I growled deeply. "Where is my witch, mutt?"

His eyes shifted. "Your witch?"

"Where. Is. She." My digits thirsted for blood.

He grew rigid. His spine straightened as he stood. "I don't know where she is." My body shook as I was on the verge of transforming once more. He quickly added, "She escaped. Knocked me on my ass after nailing me in the nuts and ran."

Pride welled in my chest, quickly followed by a pang of fear. Her screams echoed in the furthest corner of my mind.

How long has she been free from her prison? Why haven't I seen her?

I whipped around, ready to tear through the forest. "Wait! I can help!" the wolf called as he reached for me. I shoved him off, barring my temporarily human teeth.

I snarled, "Help? You've clearly *helped* enough, mongrel. Get out of my way."

"You know, you've called me about every name in the book, cat. I haven't said a godsdamned one to you," he spat. "I like to not judge a fucking book by its cover, but buddy, you are pushing it." He let out a ragged breath and his body rumbled much like my own. The hair on his arms on the verge of vibrating off of his flesh.

I turned to face him and stepped forward to where we stood chest to chest, our height almost identical. The two inches I had on the creature, I used to my advantage. I bled the promise of violence and death into my eyes as I stared down at the wolf. "I would like to make this *very* clear. If harm comes to her, if a single hair on her head is missing, you are dead. You and your entire pack. I'll enjoy every second as your blood soaks into the earth between my claws. Do you understand, *Mutt?*" He stared back as a bead of sweat dripped down the side of his face, the only sign of his fear.

Good.

"Loud and clear."

My nostril flared. "Let's go." I turned on my heel and headed north with the wolf not far behind.

Maeli, I'm coming for you.

MAELI

I woke the following morning hidden away on a semi-flat natural platform of a tree. I stumbled upon it when the moon was at its highest point in the sky; my eyes were barely open as exhaustion seeped into my bones. I half expected to have imagined the thing when I found it, perfectly hidden among a cluster of other large trees, and not a threat in sight.

I arched my back, stretching my arms above my head before I brought them back down. Bracing my hands against the bark, I twisted my torso, eliciting a few satisfying cracks from my tense spine.

I let out a quiet moan as the little bit of relief hit. Still incredibly sore, but it felt marginally better.

Perks about getting older.

I snorted halfheartedly. I barely tapped thirty-two. If I survived escaping these psychotic canines, I'd easily live well into my hundreds, maybe even hit two or three centuries before finally biting the dust.

Shaking my head to clear the barely-awake mental fog, I climbed down from my little perch. My feet thumped against the dead leaves scattered across the clover. I dusted myself off as best as I could and walked toward the patch of sunlight at the edge of the throng of oak.

There wasn't much to go by beyond the sun's position in the cloudless sky. Its heat warmed my skin as it slowly rose from the horizon, splintering shades of pink and orange as they chased away the lingering twinkle of the stars from the night before.

I glanced around, hoping to get some type of bearing on where I was. Trees in every direction. Towering mountains. The same scenery over and over again. If I weren't running for my life, it would've been calming.

But at that moment, all it did was piss me off.

"For fuck's sake!" I threw my hands in the air and kicked the dirt beneath my feet.

I clamped my eyes shut and dove inward, searching fruitlessly for my magic. If I could get it running, then I'd be able to poof myself home.

Unfortunately, I was shit out of luck. My magic remained silent. Dormant. The memory of it teased the tips of my fingers. I literally *ached*. I'd never gone that long without my magic. Even when I popped out of my deranged mother's womb, I was zapping things left and right from the get-go—much to her dismay. I scoffed at myself.

Yeah, maybe that's why she made my life hell.

Frustrated and entirely fed up, I stomped off into the wilderness ahead. There had to be an end to it somewhere.

I spent hours trekking through the undergrowth. The sun was high in the sky by the time I allowed myself to stop. The sound of water steadily flowing between cracks in the forest floor caught my attention; my throat scratched and my mouth was parched. I stumbled over my feet as I sprinted to the glistening stream. Puffs of air practically took the place of the salty sweat that drenched my dirt-covered clothes. I hadn't drank anything since I had been in my cell.

I collapsed onto the small bank with my knees sinking into the moist mud. I couldn't cup the tiny waves fast enough. Bringing the water to my lips, heavy droplets splashed between my trembling fingers, soaking the remainder of my clothes.

By the time I had my fill, I was sick to my stomach and looked like I'd just escaped being dumped into a river and left for dead. I leaned onto my back until I was flat against the riparian with my hand resting on my bulging stomach. I let out a groan. I should've paced myself.

Water poisoning is a thing.

I rolled onto my side, and the water in my belly sloshed around with the movement.

"I'm just...gonna rest...for a few," I mumbled to myself as my eyelids fluttered closed.

A growl thundered in my ears, and a wet heat beat against the side of my face. I turned my face, burying it in the crook of my arm.

Go away.

Gooey beads of grossly warm liquid plopped onto my skin. Another growl sounded.

I groggily swatted my other hand near my face. "Shoo...sleeping."

Next thing I knew, I was being slung around like a rag doll, aggressively yanking me from my slumber. My eyes shot open and I began kicking and trying to wrestle my way out of my attacker's grasp. The scent of wet dog slapped me in the face.

Crap.

I kicked my feet, landing a solid hit in the guy's throat. He coughed as he choked and dropped me. I landed with a thud and took off running.

That was too close.

My feet thumped across the ground as I ran for my life, throwing as many loops and zigzags in my trail as I could without tripping over myself. When I felt I had enough distance between the wolf and me, I found the tallest sturdiest tree I could, and began to climb. My fingers gripped the tiny notches in the bark. Pricks of wood broke against my grip as I went. My palms were clammy which made it difficult as I made my escape. I closed in on a thick branch about twenty feet off the ground and my hand slipped. I sucked in a breath and flung my body against the tree, my other hand barely hung on.

My hand began to slip.

I held my breath and hoped for the best. My stomach muscles contracted as I used my core in combination with my legs to swing my body back and forth. Just as my fingers fell from the tree, I was able to get my legs wrapped around the branch. A whoosh of air left my lungs. I shifted and pulled myself around the wood until I was sitting on top. My arms shook uncontrollably. Apparently, my muscle hadn't all gone as adrenaline worked its way through my body.

The brush below rustled as large paws thundered past only moments later. I waited with bated breath as the wolf ran by, stopping at the base of the tree to sniff then glanced around before barging into the unkept woods again.

I thanked the Gods that I'd gone rock climbing since I was a teenager. Otherwise, I never would've been able to climb the tree the way I did. I was not ready to become puppy chow quite yet.

I stayed put for about an hour until I was positive he wasn't coming back. Once the coast was clear, I quietly scurried down the long stretch of wood and hopped off at the base. glanced around and went on my way, carefully toeing through the undergrowth.

There were only two days left until Halloween. Two days until the wolves would be at their strongest. Not only would the moon be at its fullest, but it would be washed in red.

The first Blood Moon in centuries.

The effect it would have on them was unknown. It had never been recorded. The image of Maeli's body scathed and covered in her own blood, barely recognizable, flashed in my mind. My beast howled in response.

Mate. Mate. Mate.

Save her.

Kill them.

I gritted my teeth against the overwhelming urge to shift.

Not yet.

The moon had given way to the morning sun, warming my flesh as my shirt had torn the day prior.

The wolf's footing was lost on a narrow expanse, nearly costing both of us our lives had it not been for my reflexes. My shirt was destroyed in the process, but we survived.

"I'm sure we'll find her soon," the wolf said.

"If you wish to keep your soul attached to your body, we will," I growled.

He mumbled, "And I thought *wolves* had tempers." His head shook, causing his shagged red hair to swish in the breeze. "I—" He froze.

The wolf dropped to the ground, his body rippling. His slitted greys shot me a look as fur blasted across the planes of his body. I followed suit; my senses immediately on high alert.

The wet-dog scent of another wolf wafted through the air.

Followed by a familiar sweet twinge. Fear.

And an underlying hint of spice.

Maeli.

I pounced.

The tall blades of grass crunched beneath my furious paws. The small bank against the stream ahead was empty.

No!

I growled and darted forward, charging through the greenery. My nose tuned into the merging scents.

We must be close.

The russet wolf stayed on my tail, following close behind. When we came up on a massive oak, Maeli's spiced musk filled my nostrils. I inhaled until it consumed me. Motioning for the wolf to keep a lookout, I pounced onto the bark and began my ascent. The smell of her trailed the entirety of the thick trunk. My heart raced in my chest. This was it. She had to be here. Wolves are awful climbers, so she must be safe. Hidden. If she made it to the wide towering branches.

I reached the flattened heart of the tree and rapidly searched to no avail. I chirped, hoping she would hear and know it was me.

Nothing. No sound to give her away. Not even a breath of warm air. My witch was gone and out of reach. I slumped against the smooth bark, heavily resting my muzzle atop my paws. The pulsing muscle that sat between my ribs was on the verge of splitting in two, and with it, my soul.

Where is she?

The wolf barked from the base of the tree. I'd been up there long enough.

After I climbed down the wood, we paced once more, our movements slowing and on the verge of giving up all hope. My witch was lost. My Enchantress was on her own.

The wolf stopped. The realization only occurred to me due to my snout bumping against his haunches. I nipped at his fur with my fangs out. In turn, he smacked me across the face with his full tail and pointed ahead with his paw.

Twenty feet ahead of us, a form moved in the shadows. A whimper emanated from the dark figure. The sound staked my heart. The pain rang between my ears. Everything else faded away. All that was left, was *her*.

The beast faded away as I took her in my arms. She shook violently; her body was ice-cold against my own. "Maeli..." I cradled her against my bare chest, smoothing the hair on her head, whispering, "Shhh, I got you, sweetheart. I'm here."

Her teeth chattered. "Al-Alastor?"

I tilted her head up to face me and brushed my thumb along the edge of her chin. "I'm here." A single tear slid down her cheek.

Her bottom lip wobbled. Our eyes locked and blood thundered in my ears. My heart thundered in my chest.

My mate.

Our lips crashed together.

All the missing pieces in my chest clicked together. Relief washed over every inch of my body, and inter-twined with every fiber of my being.

Embers sparked between us. Within moments, we were enveloped in the flames of our connection. She was mine and I was hers. Forever.

Until the end of time.

"Hey, uh, hate to break up this little lust-fest, but we might want to get out of here."

Maeli jumped, startled in my arms by the disruption. Our kiss broke and I shot a glare at the wolf.

"We got company." The wolf threw his thumb up, motioning toward the rustling bush line.

We swore collectively. The wolf and I shifted and Maeli stood shaking. I knocked my head to the side and she climbed onto the wolf's back, much to my dismay.

She'll have a better grip.

The beast grunted in response. I shoved his disdain along with my own away and we were off, racing through the forest.

A distant howl sounded behind us, completely abandoned in our wake and we kicked up our speed. The woodland flew past, thinning as we escaped the forest.

We came upon another stream and hurdled through the water, being sure to douse ourselves in it, so our scents were whisked away by the small current. At least, that was the intent.

An abandoned cabin stood broken a mile further, just on the outskirts of the forest edge.

Maeli slid down the wolf's back as we came to a halt. Her pale olive fingers brushed against the wolf's fur, lingering, as she muttered an apology.

The beast within me lunged forth. My paws heavy against the dirt as I wedged between the wolf and my witch.

Mate.

Mine.

The beast within me growled with claws extended a mere inch from the wolf's flank.

Maeli stepped between as trickles of fear dimmed in her eyes. Hot anger flared beneath the surface. "Alastor!" she hissed. "Stop!"

I swung my head in her direction, snapping my jowls shut to keep myself from barring my fangs.

"Good." She flicked my nose and the wolf snickered. She whirled around on him. "Don't egg him on!"

I bit back my own feline cackle and nudged her shoulder. She shook her head, muttering under her breath, and padded into the decrepit shack. I followed behind while the wolf stood guard outside.

The moment the wood-planked door creaked shut behind us, my witch turned, and her arms quickly wrapped around me.

My body shifted, returning to my human form. I covered her frame and circled my arms around her waist as I pulled her into my lap. A low purr vibrated in my chest as I nuzzled the top of her head, burying myself in her natural musk.

"Maeli," I groaned her name into the matted trundles of her hair.

My witch.

My heart clenched. She was finally in my arms again; finally out of harm's way.

She wriggled in my embrace, twisting until she faced me, our eyes locking. She reached up, cupping my cheek in her hand. Her irises glistened in the broken moonlight streaking in through the cracked walls. I sighed into her touch and turned to place a kiss in her palm.

Maeli grinned, her soft smile warming the small space. I leaned down, resting my forehead against hers. My breath hitched. "May I kiss you?"

She squeaked out a yes and our lips clashed together. My arms further tightened around her as our kiss deepened.

Lips parting, tongues danced. Our hands roamed one another as the hunger between us, the hunger of being separated for so many months, dug in its ravenous claws.

I growled as her nails dragged along my back. Warm trickles of blood dripped from the toe-curling lacerations. She moaned as my hardening length twitched between us. My shaft eagerly pressed against her center through the fabric of her clothing.

I needed her body closer to mine. To feel her warmth and her heat wet against my own. I gripped her shirt, ripping it in two. My hands roamed her flesh, popping open the clasp of her bra along the way.

My hands dropped to her hips, lifting her body so I could taste the plump tips of her breasts. She moaned as I swirled my tongue around the delicious mound, eliciting a matching groan from deep within me.

I hoisted her up higher until her sweet dripping cunt was within reach. Her legs wrapped around me as her wetness beaconed me, begging to be devoured.

I blew hot air across her aching center. She shuttered, instantly pebbling her skin. I flicked my tongue between her folds slowly, savoring each drop of her nectar. Reaching her clit, I swirled my tongue around the sensitive mound, nipping and sucking as I went.

I feasted on her center, drinking every drop of her.

My tongue darted in and out of her folds. I slid one hand away from her hips, the other pressed against the base of her spine to hold her delicious body in place.

"Alastor!" she cried out as my fingers dipped into her warmth. I pumped my digit in and out, then slipped in another and then another until she was near bursting.

I gently brought her down, lying her on the ground with her beautifully intoxicating body on full display. I kissed her inner thigh, trailing my way up to the apex. I flicked my tongue against her bundle of nerves at the center before continuing my trail along her delicate lush skin.

I pulled her nipple between my teeth, nipping lightly. Maeli squealed in response as her body wriggled beneath mine.

My cock twitched between us.

Maeli lifted her body, trying to create some friction. I flayed my fingers against her soft stomach, pressing her body down. The primal beast inside crawled its way out and purred into her flesh, "Tell me how much you need my cock buried deep in your wet pussy."

"Please!" she cried out, her breath heavy. "Alastor, I need you. Please!" She arched her back, and the heat of her naked skin pressed against me.

Nipping at her exposed neck, my words caressed her sensitive flesh. "Such a good girl, Maeli." I bit down, sucking at her neck until I felt the pops of her tiny veins, marking her. "Such a good fucking *witch*."

I lined the head of my cock up with her entrance

and pushed forward. My hard length slid in until I reached the hilt. We let out a groan simultaneously as I filled her completely. She was so tight, so wet. Made for me.

"You take me so well, Maeli."

Take us *so well.*

I took her lips with mine and pounded into her. Each thrust, harder, deeper. She cried out, begging for release.

Powerfully thrusting into her tight pussy until she clenched around me, and her body began to shake as her orgasm washed over her, my own not far behind. Her breasts heaved with each shagged breath as she came down from her climax. Her hair flowed in wild waves around her face. Sweat slicked her skin and pooled in her midsection. Our satisfaction swirled together as I gently pulled myself from her cunt, oozing onto the floor below our flushed bodies.

I lay next to her, pulling her body against mine with my arm circling her waist as I clung to her. Maeli rolled and buried her face in my chest. I nestled my nose into her hair, breathing her in. She let out a contented sigh and quickly drifted off to sleep. Within moments, I too drifted off, my dreams filled with my witch.

Safe in my arms once more.

❧ 6 ☙

MAELI

I found him. I'd found Alastor.

After months of being held hostage, and a good couple of days scrambling through miles of dense woods, there he was.

Okay, he found me. But still.

The second he had me and I realized he wasn't one of the wolves trying to hunt and murder me, the pressure in my chest disappeared. The emptiness I'd been feeling for months was gone.

And my magic...she was there. Humming. Waiting. I could feel it.

We came undone together. And so did whatever had my magic bound.

I was free.

I woke up to sunlight blasting me in the face and Alastor's hot breath on my skin. I shifted in his arms and he let out a little moan. Stifling back a giggle, I draped my leg over his.

His cock twitched against my exposed center, sending a shiver down my spine. I licked my lips and peppered his chest with kisses before rolling him onto his back as my hips straddled his thighs. His dick was as huge and delicious as I remembered. I smirked.

He's so hard so early in the morning, I might as well call him Woody.

My fingers lightly poked the head, seeing if that would probe my sleeping panther awake. No such luck. I pouted and started to gently swirl my pointer finger around the tip. He continued to breathe heavily, still sound asleep.

My hand slid to his shaft, gliding down and back up, squeezing near the top, just how he liked all those months ago. I'd figured it out after our joint romance reading session. *That* was a fun one.

His member twitched in my hand.

Wake up dammit!

I leaned down and took him into my mouth. I started slowly with my tongue licking the tip, lapping up the bead of precum oozing from it. I moaned at his taste and took him further between my lips. I stroked his cock in time with my mouth with one hand on his thick shaft, the other massaging his balls.

"Maeli…" Alastor groaned.

Excitement bubbled up in my chest. He was finally awake.

I picked up my pace, taking him deeper, tears welling at the corners of my eyes as his huge cock hit the back of my throat. He stroked my hair, twirling it until he could grab it with his fist then pulled.

His cock sprang from my lips with a loud pop as saliva drooled down the corners. "My, my. Such a beautiful way to be woken." He leaned forward in the most graceful way I'd ever seen, released my hair from his grip, and took my chin between his thumb and forefinger. "Wouldn't you say, *Enchantress?*" He licked his lips as a dark hunger lit up his eyes.

I swallowed heavily as my mouth watered.

His eyes traveled down my still very naked body before meeting mine. My core melted under his heated gaze. "Such a dirty witch." He kissed the sensitive spot on my neck. "Be a good girl, and stand up for me."

I did as he said. The fire in his eye bore into me. I began to squirm under his gaze. The delicious tension caused a roar between my legs. Alastor smirked as he positioned himself underneath me, spreading my very damp thighs and exposing me so that his face was in the perfect position to be ridden. I waited with bated breath. My eyes clamped shut, unable to shove down the excitement tumbling in my stomach. I needed him. I needed his tongue on me, tasting me, devouring me until I came all over his handsome face and then some. I needed him to ruin me.

A few moments passed, and no touch. No contact. It drove me nuts. "Alastor, please. I need you."

He chuckled lowly. "Do you? Tell me, Enchantress. What *do* you need?" His breath was hot on my bare skin. I whimpered. "Do you want me to touch you?" The tip of his finger brushed my thigh. "Taste you?" His tongue flicked the spot behind my knee. "Do you want my cock buried deep inside you?" He breathed into the base of my spine. "My seed pulsing and filling your cunt?" He licked between my shoulder blades. His hand palmed my breast, massaging its fullness. "Or do you wish for me to mark you? Ruin you and claim you so no man, no male, shall ever lay their hands on you again." His lips went to my throat.

"You are mine and mine alone, Enchantress. Death will meet the fate of anyone who dares to touch you or take you from me again. And I will claim you over and over again in their wake, in the blood of those who hurt you. No one will come between us again."

His words clenched around my beating heart, unlocking something dark within me. Primal.

My eyes shot open and I turned on him, tackling him to the ground. My magic roared to life. Alastor's hands were all over my body and mine over his. I clawed into his skin as the heat between my thighs became unbearable. His mouth latched onto my flesh, sucking and licking until he released with a pop and continued the action until he reached my breasts. He yanked me down so they smothered him. One hand squeezed and pinched my taught mound at the center of my breast while his tongue attacked the other.

I swirled my hips against his length, hot, hard, and massive. Everything was on fire. He growled and pressed his cock against my clit, harder, and grinded with me. My body shook as my orgasm climbed, taking me higher until I exploded. I roared and fell against Alastor as my breath became labored.

"We're not done yet, Enchantress," he whispered into my ear.

Alastor lifted my still burning body and brought me down on his cock, slamming into my cervix. "Oh Gods, Maeli...you feel so good." I moaned as he pumped into me. My head snapped back as another wave of please built, thrusting my chest further against his hungry lips.

My magic erupted, and my orgasm crested with it. My body shook from the onslaught and I collapsed in Alastor's arms. He peppered kisses along my overly sensitive skin, reaching for my lips last. He locked his with mine in a long, exhausted, passion-filled kiss and slowly, gently, laid me on my back.

Alastor smoothed my without-a-doubt sex-crazed mane. The chocolates of his eyes twinkled in the early light as I admired his touch. A peaceful calm blanketed the cabin. "Every part of me is yours, Enchantress."

He planted a kiss on top of my head and I drifted off to sleep.

7
ALASTOR

Maeli fell into a blissful sleep. Her hair framed her angelic face. Her cheeks were shaded a bright pink as if kissed by a frosted night.

I rolled away from her warmth and quietly padded outside, stretching in the fall sun.

My head shot up at a grating cough.

The wolf sat hunched over with his hands shoved between his legs, probably in an attempt to keep them warm.

"You stayed in human form all night?" I asked.

He shook his head. "No. I uh, heard you guys and changed back. Didn't feel like playing the creepy spectator to your hump fest."

I scoffed.

Imagine that, a canine with some manners.

"Apologizes, wolf. Nearly a year apart from one's mate can do that."

He humphed. "Simon."

"Pardon me?"

"My name. It's Simon. So, you can stop calling me 'wolf' or whatever derogatory names you've got on your tongue." He sighed and leaned against the cabin. "I helped get your girl out. It's all I ask."

I stared for a moment. "Alright."

"I can't exactly go back, ya know. They'll smell her on me. And you. They'll kill me for helping you two."

"And why is that my problem?"

A stick thunked against my skull.

"I'd prefer to keep my pelt. I don't exactly agree with the rest of them and this bullshit just proved it." Simon blew out a puff of air. "The whole kill-first-ask-questions-later thing ain't for me. I've seen enough of it."

"Join the club." Maeli's melodious voice followed her over the cabin's threshold. She plopped down on my right, placing herself between us. "So, what's the real reason you let me go, Wolfie?" She tossed the stick to him, or rather...she tried. The thin wood landed in the opposite direction.

Simon's brow shot up. "How'd you know?"

"A powerless witch out maneuvering a new wolf? That's easily double my size? I might've been too hopped up on adrenaline at the time but I'm not dumb enough to think I'm *that* lucky."

"Could've fooled me."

"Yeah, well, it took me a bit to come to the realization. Kinda pieced it together when you showed up with this lug." Maeli jutted her thumb toward me. "It helped that you didn't try to claw my brains out, too."

Simon shrugged. "Shredded brains don't taste that great."

A growl vibrated in my belly.

I will end you.

Simon snickered and rolled his eyes. "Oh, don't get your nuts in a twist. I'm screwing around."

I snapped my jaws at the wolf, allowing my fangs to phase out.

Maeli stood and my eyes widened.

She was completely bare. The image of shredding her clothes the night before flashed through my mind.

Dammit.

I shot to my feet, throwing myself in front of her and she pushed me away as confusion plastered her features. "What the hell are you doing, Alastor?"

My gaze traveled her body before meeting her hazel eyes. She glanced down, and her eyes widened as realization struck her. She snapped her attention to me as a beet-red blush quickly spread across her cheeks and down her neck before covering her skin entirely.

Maeli squeaked, "Shit!" Then bolted inside, scavenging for any cloth she could find. She groaned in frustration when she came up short.

"You ain't my type, Short stack. No need to be

embarrassed around me," Simon shouted from where he lounged in the dirt. My body shook, ready to claw the male's throat out for laying his eyes on my mate. Regardless of his attraction. She was *mine*.

"Ugh!" She stomped her foot into the floor. "Wait a second—" Her voice cut off. Panic seized me. I ripped what had remained of the door off of its hinges as my chest heaved.

Maeli let out a scream and threw something at my head. No—zapped something at me. "Don't scare me like that, asshole!"

"You...I thought something happened."

She threw her hands on her hips as an angry pout appeared. It was utterly adorable.

"My magic came back. I was zapping some clothes on." She tapped her foot. "It...uh...came back this morning...when we, uh...ya know..." An alluring blush slowly crept up her neck, flushing her cheeks. Her heated complexion sent a jolt of arousal to my cock.

I quickly bound across the cabin, cupping her chin between my thumb and forefinger. My baritone voice purred along her skin. "Oh, I know exactly when it returned, Enchantress." Goosebumps rose along her delicate skin with each word. "After all these months, I could finally breathe you in. Sense you. *Every intoxicating part of you.*" I brought my lips a mere breath away from hers. "You are *my mate*, after all."

Her pupils blew, and an 'o' formed on her lips. "M-mate?"

"Well of course, dearest."

She pulled her bottom lip between her teeth, worrying it back and forth. Her eyes left mine, and the redness of her cheeks deepened. "I-I—woah." Her fingers twitched. "I just thought you were really...uh... really *hot*."

I chuckled. "My being easy on the eyes helped, I imagine. But, yes, Maeli. You are mine and I am yours. If you'll have me."

"I-I—" she stammered.

A loud bang sounded outside.

Simon poked his head in. "Hey, uh, hate to break up this whole love confession shindig but we got company."

We both swore and ran out the door. Maeli threw her hands out to her sides while I shifted into my beast.

❧ 8 ❧

MAELI

Mate.

He said I'm his mate.

I briefly remembered Alastor calling me his mate while we were in the throws of heated sex, but it didn't fully register.

How is this even possible?

Witches didn't have "mates." Could we find someone and settle down? Of course, but we didn't have *soulmates.* Those were reserved for shifters and the occasional shifter-human hybrid. And sure, there were kids whose parents were from different creatures and species...but they weren't *mates.* And their kids didn't get any of their abilities or powers. The supernatural powers always ended with the parents in those rare instances.

What if he wanted kids? They wouldn't have any of

this. We'd have to keep our lives secret from them. They wouldn't be able to know.

Sure, I've been dreaming of Alastor and getting all hot and bothered for months on end, but I assumed that was pent up sexual frustration from being held hostage in a cemented dirt block against my will. I never would've thought we were *mates*.

OH my Gods.

My magic.

The way it responded to him. The humming. The sudden onslaught after being drugged for so long and having it stripped of me.

Crap.

A chorus of howling wolves shook the trees, breaking my train of thought. They were catching up. I needed to get my head out of my ass and focus on getting us out of here.

Alastor and Simon ran along each side of me. I threw my hands out, twirling my wrists as I called my magic.

Transport.

A cloud of shimmering grey poofed twenty feet ahead. "Jump in! Hurry!" I shouted, picking up my own speed. Simon dove through first. I yelled for Alastor to jump ahead of me so I could make sure he made it before closing the portal.

He whined in protest, skidding to a halt.

"Dammit, Alastor! I need you to go first! I'll be right behind you!" I pushed his flank, trying to urge him forward. He snapped at me and wrapped his massive jowls around my waist before leaping through the grey mist. I wriggled in his grasp, needing to see to close our escape. I peaked around finally, and screamed. An entire pack of wolves, easily reaching the double digits, were hot on our tails. I waved my hands, and the portal closed inch by painstakingly slow inch.

The wolves were a mere ten feet away as the final gap slowly closed. A loud bone-shattering cackle sounded from the other side, and a flash of shimmering yellowish-white skirted the edges. The portal snapped shut, nicking a fleck of the shimmery dread-inducing material.

It drifted into the palms of my frozen hands.

The material...was hair.

Blonde *golden* hair.

No. There's no possible way.

Except...it was possible. Very, nerve-rackingly possible.

"Mother."

It left my lips, barely a whisper, but the word roared in my ears like a tsunami's waves.

Alastor said something, but the world around me was too deafening.

My mother—she wanted to kill me.

Well. That sure puts a damper on things.

❧ 9 ❧

ALASTOR

aeli's face paled. Terror filled her eyes. Her heart rate quickened as if she were a rabbit up for slaughter with a wolf at her neck.

The latter may have been accurate unfortunately, however, she was no hare.

She lay in my bed in shock. Somehow, the portal she'd drawn had taken us to my apartment, to which I hadn't been since the day she disappeared. Maeli had never set foot in here either.

Interesting.

I shooed the wolf away as my attention, every nerve in my body, tuned into my witch. "Maeli?"

She mumbled a response. Her gaze clouded and locked on the ceiling.

"I'm sorry, my love, I didn't understand. What did

you say?" I asked gently, brushing a loose hair from her furrowed brow.

"My mother. She wants to kill me." Emotion void, her words a pure fact.

I blinked. "Your mother?"

She held up the palm of her hand, and in it sat a tiny yellowed speck. I squinted, trying to figure out what it was.

"I saw her, heard her. She was with them. With the pack."

"Why would she want to hurt you?" I worriedly questioned. My own parents and I strongly disagreed but not to the point of murder.

Maeli was silent with her mouth pressed into a thin line.

I sat with her, stroking her hair, and rubbing her soft stomach. My mate was being hunted by her own flesh and blood.

After a while, the tension in her body wavered and she leaned into my touch. Her shoulders shook as silent cries fell from the corners of her eyes.

"Hush, my love. I won't let her hurt you," I whispered as I bent forward and placed a kiss on her damp cheek.

We spent the remainder of the day cuddled up on my bed, hidden from the terror stalking us. Simon clanked around in the kitchen, scavenging for scraps to toss together for a meal.

Early evening came, along with a crockpot of chicken casserole, and I carried Maeli to my kitchen, setting her in the head chair at my table. My strong, feisty witch was deflated, and a wave of resignation swallowed her.

Simon must've noticed as well. "I had no idea Ravenna was your mom, Maeli. I'm so sorry."

An icy tundra encapsulated my insides. "Ravenna?" Simon nodded as bleakness crowded the silver of his eyes. I pressed my lips together.

Ravenna was the name of the individual I'd been tracking before Maeli disappeared. The one the SDWS had thought to be at the center of the werewolf attacks —all the violence. The core of the movement who was trying to expose the supernatural to the humans before eradicating them.

I turned to Maeli, forcing the fear below the surface. "Ravenna is your mother?"

Maeli nodded as her swollen eyes filled with tears once more. "Unfortunately."

"Damn. That sucks." I shot Simon a glare, barring my teeth in the process. The wolf's days were becoming limited. He rolled his eyes in response. "Must've been such a fun childhood."

Maeli pointed her finger at him and sent a spark flying. The little jolt of electricity smacked Simon right in the center of his chest, causing him to jerk in his seat. The darkness that had crept across her lifted ever so slightly, and a small smirk played at the corner of her plush pouted lips.

I glanced between the two, unsure. Perhaps he had the ability to pull her from this stupor, something I seemed to be lacking. Envious green tendrils sliced their way across the fabric of my heart. I bit my tongue, ignoring the bite of jealous hatred.

She couldn't love him. Not with a mate bond.

The Gods wouldn't allow it.

Maeli broke my train of thought. "She saw me as competition. And I guess, now she's ready to get rid of me for good. She finally snapped."

I paused, fury licked at my core.

"Maeli, do you know *why* your mother would want you dead?"

Maeli rolled her head in my direction, irritation in place of the defeat from moments before. She dead-panned, "I just said. Competition. Insanity. Snapping? Keep up."

Simon sighed and propped his arm beneath his chin as he leaned onto the table. "She's crazy all right, but it's more than that, babe." We both shot him another look, hers confused, mine a promised threat.

Maeli's eyes narrowed and her teeth clicked together. "Do. Not. Call. Me. Babe."

"Won't happen again, sorry." Simon tossed his hands up in defense. "But gotta break up the doom and gloom somehow, and getting under Kitty's skin here seems like a fun way to go about it."

I ignored him and laid it all out for her. "The case I was working on, Maeli, as your furry friend just informed me, she's behind it. And with that being the case...for what she's planning, she needs a sacrifice." I gulped. "You're it."

Maeli's eyes widened. "Sacrifice? For what? Since when is this the 1800s?"

I breathed a brief sigh of relief, at least Maeli had no knowledge of it. The SDWS wouldn't be able to accuse her of conspiracy—if we could keep her alive.

"Tomorrow is a Blood Moon."

She cocked her brow. "Your point?"

I sighed a steadying breath, needing to maintain a level head. "It's the first one to fall on All Hallows' Eve in centuries. The first one that will have a recorded history." My gaze slid to the wolf, and my beast growled in my skull in warning. "Starting with the wolves. And then the other shifters: witches, vampires, selkies, and all the creatures in between."

"My kind will be the strongest, along with the witches," Simon added. "Hence, Ravenna's purpose for shacking up with the wolves. Under any other circumstances, they'd be ripping each other apart, with your mother at the forefront. If she didn't need us, we'd be her first victims since wolves and shifters are her biggest threat aside from the humans."

"But why would she need the wolves? That doesn't make any sense. We've been at each other's throats for eons at this point." The wheels of Maeli's mind spun quickly.

"Beats me. Either way, she needs us. And you. The sacrifice needed to be a very powerful, pure-blooded witch. You fit the bill." He shrugged. "As your feline boyfriend conceded, tomorrow's dooms day. Which is why I'm here. We keep you out of momsie's hands and the wolves' paws, and presto, no all powerful supernatural exposures to the very scared and violent human population."

I narrowed my eyes. "What's in it for you, Wolf?"

"Hey, we agreed, no more little names." Simon tossed up a finger gun and clicked his tongue.

"You referred to me as, 'Kitty.'" I clenched my jaw, fully over the game he was playing.

"Fair enough." Simon waved his hand in the air. "I just want out of this mess and to live a quiet life. Maybe shack up with some spunky little human." A toothy grin spread from cheek to cheek, causing the silver in his eyes to twinkle. "Perhaps that spunky friend of yours, Witchling." He winked.

And signed his death wish.

Maeli shot out of her chair, sending it flying backwards and splintering into thousands of pieces as it connected with my antique hutch. Simon flew into the air as his fingers grasped at his neck, gasping for air. "Leave Kali out of this, dog," she growled. "How long did Ravenna have you watching me?"

"She...didn't," he choked out. Maeli squeezed her

hand, constricting the magical grip further. His flesh began to turn a shade of purple.

A spark of satisfaction lit within me.

Then reality sunk in. We needed Simon.

"Maeli, put him down." I stepped forward slowly, not wanting to be next on her list. Kali was her best friend and a bit of a sensitive spot.

Her arm shot out, palm facing me. I stopped in my tracks.

"Nobody moves." She released her magic from Simon's neck. He dropped to the floor, gasping for breath. One of my chef's knives came flying from a drawer. It halted with the tip poking into his skin, pressed against his windpipe. "You tell a single white hair of a lie and your head is mine, Mutt. How do you know about Kali and what is she to you?"

"O-okay." The Adam's apple of his neck bobbed. "It was after the others napped you. Ravenna sent me to scout and be sure that the wolf that captured you hadn't left any direct trails to their caverns. I'd spotted her from the trees surrounding your little slice of paradise. Nice place by the way. Small but nice—" The knife edged inward.

"Get on with it!"

"Sorry! I saw her and she took my breath away. Most beautiful woman, especially human woman, I'd ever lay my eyes on." His breathing slowed. "I followed her and stuck around, out of sight for a few, until I was able to break the ice and introduce myself.

She went into some gym and so I made my move there."

Maeli rolled her eyes and scoffed. "Why is it always the gym? Can't a woman workout in peace?"

My beast snickered.

Silence.

Simon continued, "Look, it just seemed like a normal public place. I went up to her and asked to grab a cup of coffee." He sighed, a hint of disappointment in his expression. "She turned me down and told me to get lost."

Maeli threw her hands on her hips. "Well, there's your answer, Simon. She said no, so leave her out of it."

"You don't understand! I *can't*, Maeli."

"Uh, yeah, you can. She said, no. That's that. I will cut you."

He glanced over at me, silently pleading. My brows arched in surprise.

Isn't this interesting?

I just may see a wolf skinned by my witch's hand today.

"Alastor, help a guy out. Tell her. Please!"

Maeli whirled her head around to glare at me, betrayal in her hazel eyes. "Excuse me? Tell me what?"

I feigned innocence. "I'm not sure what the wolf is referring to, dearest."

She narrowed her eyes. "Alastor."

I shrugged my shoulders. This was the wolf's battle, not my own.

Maeli snapped her fingers and the words tumbled from my lips. "They're mates."

Red-hot rage filled her face. Maeli wielded the chef's knife with an expert witch's hand and sliced into Simon's flesh. Unfortunately, she avoided his jugular, and instead, made her mark on his chest. "*Mates? Are you serious right now?*"

Simon nodded sheepishly. "I can't exactly control this stuff."

Maeli scoffed. "No fucking shit." My eyes widened. "This whole mate business is a mess—" She glanced my way. "Alastor, don't you even dare start any of that over-thinking, spiraly stuff. Me and you, we're good." I released a breath and her attention returned to Simon. "I'm talking about the Gods just throwing them around all willy-nilly. A wolf and a human make as much sense as a witch and a shifter. Again, we're fine, Alastor. Just using an example."

Relief flooded my system knowing I hadn't terrified her as much as I had thought.

Maeli's foot tapped rapidly on the linoleum while she sorted her thoughts.

"Alright, fine. I'll help. I'm not forcing her hand because she should have a damn choice in this. But I won't stand in the way if you want to try introducing yourself again. *But that is it.* I'm not forcing the only family into something they want no part of. And neither are you, do you understand? You harm a single hair on her little human head and I will destroy you. Balls first.

I'll chop them off with a dull plastic spoon and shove them down your throat before slicing this knife up your dick and down the whole of your body. Got it?"

We both shivered at the image. His expression was full of fear. Mine was pure pride at the lengths my witch was willing to go for her friend. There was no doubt in my mind that my Enchantress was made for me.

10

MAELI

I was over all of it.

I mulled over the certain death we would be facing. *I* would be facing. It was the final countdown without the kickass music. Death at my doorstep. Literally, since I'd transported us again, only this time to my own little hidden cottage.

It had felt good to be home if only for the briefest moment. A hint of pine and cedar wafted throughout my cottage with a hint of allspice lingering at the edges. Not a speck of dust in sight, and my books remained in perfect condition; even new releases were added to the shelves.

As if reading my mind, Alastor walked up behind me and wrapped his arms around my waist. "I took care of your shop and the cottage while you were gone. It was difficult, given I hunted for you nearly every waking hour, but Kali was a wonderful help."

A warm fuzzy feeling crawled up my insides, settling in my chest, bringing with it a content smile. The calm before the storm.

If I survive this, I'm unhexing her espresso machine.

Actually, no, I'll get her a brand-spankin'-new one.

The jitters were getting to me. Outside of our little sweet moment, I couldn't sit still. I ran around my house reorganizing the place: moving cups, sliding rugs around, and cleaned out the pantry three different times. Arranging my stock twice and my bedroom once. Simon took up shop on the couch while Alastor followed me around, helping where he could and doing every ludicrous request I had.

It was after midnight by the time he got me to sit still for more than point five seconds. Alastor stopped me midstep with his hand lightly touching my shoulder.

I turned, looking up at his tall muscular frame and he pulled me into him, nearly crushing me in the process. I wrapped my arms around him, squeezing with all the pent up fear and anger that pulsed through me. Silent tears finally came crashing down. It was all too much. I'd gotten out from under my mother's abusive controlling thumb only to be dragged back against my will and waiting at the gallows.

I sucked in a shaking breath and whispered a promise into Alastor's toned stomach. "I won't go down without a fight."

He leaned down and kissed the top of my head. "We'll be in this together. I'll be right by your side. If we die trying to keep Ravenna and her followers from destroying everything, we die together."

I pulled back, and our eyes met. His were the most delicious chocolate, shimmering in the dimmed lights in my bedroom. My heart clenched in my chest. He really was my mate. I could feel it in my bones, humming through my magic. I was made for him and he was made for me. For this moment. What we were about to face, we were created for this.

I stood on the tips of my toes. Alastor leaned forward to meet me and our lips touched, slowly working together, savoring what might be our last time together.

Our hands explored one another's bodies tenderly, lingering. His fingers curled in my hair, gently pulling my head back, exposing my neck. Alastor trailed kisses from my chin to the top of my chest, each more tender than the last. He brought his other hand down my spine, cupping my ass before circling around and sliding his hand between my legs.

He dipped one large finger between my slick center, pressing it deep and curling inward. My legs quaked beneath me, giving out as he slipped a second finger inside. He expertly stroked my insides until I was coming undone with his thumb at my clit, circling it in conjunction with the thrusts. I moaned as my orgasm crested.

Alastor took my mouth in his after sucking my juices off his digits, allowing me to taste myself on his tongue. Our kiss deepened, eliciting a groan from him. His hands circled around, cupping my ass again and hoisted me up. He lined his cock with my mid-air pussy and dove in, pounding into my wetness, wearing my pussy like a tailor-made glove. My ass smacked against his sack as we moved faster and faster, the need between us beyond desperate.

"Maeli—" he chanted my name with each thrust. The sound of my name on his lips drove me over my limit, and another climax tore into me. I moaned his name in return, my body shaking. His release quickly followed, his seed filling my center and oozing out.

As we came down from our euphoric two-person tango, he walked us to my bed and collapsed onto the down covers, wrapping me against his chest as we disregarded our impending doom for the night.

❧ **II** ❧

ALASTOR

ll Hallows' Eve.

The day was here, or rather, the night.

Maeli and I stood hand in hand in the forest outside of her cottage. Simon stood to her left, already in wolf form. I'd opted to wait to shift until I could no longer, needing to feel my witch's hand in mine.

Her power was immense, even more so under the Blood Moon. The wind moved around us, flowing through her. As if she were able to control the element herself; as if she and the air were one in the same.

Branches crashed half a mile away.

My beast growled and my body shifted. My panther was ready to come out and play. We braced ourselves. It was time.

The moon was high in the sky, overlooking our

celestial   powered,   soon-to-be-crimson-covered, battlefield.

Howls crested over the line of trees, stirring the resting birds within the canopies.

They were here.

❧ 12 ❧

MAELI

A pack of ten oversized monster wolves padded into the clearing. At the center, my mother—Ravenna. She wore a smirk on her dark, ageless magic-enhanced face. Witches lived for a while, but we weren't immortal. Not naturally.

One's soul had to pretty much be sold and lean heavily on dark magic to obtain it. And, to no surprise, my evil witch of a mother seems to have done exactly that. Which also meant, our chances of defeating her just fell drastically. Blood Moon plus an already powerful witch with dark magic at her beck and call…

We were royally fucked.

Her holier-than-thou voice rang out, "Maeli, my dear child! Mommy's missed you, my dear little witch."

I spat.

"Tut-tut. Still no manners, I see." Judgment oozed from her as she gave Alastor's panther the up down. "To be expected, I suppose. Shacking up with a panther. Here I thought I'd raised you better than that." She shook her head, her blonde curls bouncing with the movement. "Alas, it matters not." She snapped her fingers. The wolf she rode on dipped its neck, allowing her to climb down. "Are you ready to die?"

She asked so...calmly. How a normal person would ask about the weather.

I crossed my arms over my chest. "Mother. Here I thought someone as powerful and all-knowing such as yourself would know the answer to that." I plastered on a shit-eating grin. "You and your mutt army can go fuck yourselves."

Ravenna huffed and waved her fingers through the air. A burst of wind barreled toward us, quickly followed by half of the pack heavy on their paws.

This was it. It was now or never.

I threw my arms out, mustering together all the magic I could. My eyes squeezed shut as I dove inward, searching for more and more energy—more power. My magic flourished, fluttering about as if it had been waiting. It hummed to life, erupting from my finger tips.

My mother's wind was forced back and her wolves went flying, whimpering as they were flung against bark and trunks of massive oaks. Ravenna roared, and flames rushed toward us. Alastor jumped in front of me, shielding my body from the overbearing heat. The furious fire kept growing, burning everything around us. Simon howled out in pain. I quickly glanced his way. A wolf had made it through and tore into Simon's flank.

"Alastor, you need to go help him!" I shouted over the roaring flames. He shook his head, refusing to move. "Alastor!" He stood his ground. The fire was getting closer.

I'm sorry.

I squeezed my eyes closed and sent my powers out to him, lifting him and forcing him to Simon. Alastor growled in protest, his paws batting at the air. I threw up a wall once he was on the ground, keeping him from running back to me. We could still see each other, but his paws were forced. He was going to keep Simon alive. He could be pissed at me later.

"My, my. You think you're so powerful, don't you?" Ravenna taunted. "Well, sugar, I hate to break it to you, but you are *nothing* compared to me." She cackled and power released from her outspread bony fingers.

"I don't think, *Mother*. I know." I held my own digits outward, stopping her tidal wave of deadly destruction in its wake and shoving it back toward her. Her wolves stood no chance. The ones that remained shattered into furred dust, their blood sputtering in the deadly breeze.

Ravenna, however, was nowhere to be found.

Gonna stick a pin in that one for later.

I ran to Alastor and Simon, dropping the clear wall between us. "Are you guys okay?"

Simon's wolf limped before flopping on the ground with a huff.

Alastor shifted back, his human form whisking me into his strong hold. "We're fine." He inhaled sharply. "Don't ever do that again, Maeli."

"No promises," I said, my voice muffled by his bare chest.

"Did we get them all?" Simon asked, exasperated having shifted to his own human body.

"All but *her*."

"I have a feeling that won't be the last we see of Ravenna."

My gut wrenched, and with it, my magic. This wasn't over.

"I think you might be right."

Simon coughed from his spot on the dirt. "Hey, we survived. And you know what—" Another cough. "This little bloodied pow-wow was pretty witchin'." He tried to smirk and it failed.

Alastor and I both shook our heads at our new ally's humor. Each of us shouldered Simon's body and carried him back to my cottage.

We survived.

For now.

Book Two

End

ACKNOWLEDGMENTS

First of all, I want to give a huge thanks to you for reading *Have A Witchin' Howl-O-Ween*! It seriously means a lot! Thank you to my readers and my street team! You are freaking rockstars!

Secondly, thank you to my editor for putting up with me. They're the absolute best!

To my spouse, thank you so much for always supporting me and encouraging me to keep writing and bouncing some of these awful puns off of each other. And for not batting an eye when I text you in the middle of the night with some random out-of-context snippet for feedback or just because I'm kicking my feet excited as all hell over the tiniest little piece of writing from the day (or night because what the frickity-frack is sleep?).

To my grandparents, for raising me to always chase my dreams and for always being supportive of every-thing I do. They're my best friends (in addition to my spouse) and I wouldn't be here without them.

To my best friend who reads everything I write, your support...dude it's incredible. You're the coolest cat around.

A Series of Smutacular Witchy Shifter Novellas

Have A Holly Jolly Shiftmas (Book One)

Have A Witchin' Howl-O-Ween (Book Two)

Standalone's

Suck Me Harder: A Smutty Vampire Romance Novella

FOLLOW ON SOCIAL MEDIA

Instagram - @author.s.p.icey

Facebook - Author S. P. Icey

https://snowpirebooksllc.myshopify.com/